Florence Robinson

THE STORY OF A JAZZ AGE GIRL

by Dorothy and Thomas Hoobler
in conjunction with Carey-Greenberg Associates
illustrations by Robert Sauber

SILVER BURDETT PRESS
Parsippany, New Jersey

Published by Silver Burdett Press
A Division of Simon & Schuster
299 Jefferson Road, Parsippany, New Jersey 07054

Designed by JP Design Associates

Manufactured in the United States of America
ISBN 0-382-39644-8 (LSB) 10 9 8 7 6 5 4 3 2 1
ISBN 0-382-39645-6 (PBK) 10 9 8 7 6 5 4 3 2 1

Library of Congress Cataloging-in-Publication Data
Hoobler, Dorothy
Florence Robinson: the story of a jazz age girl/by Dorothy and
Thomas Hoobler and Carey-Greenberg Associates; illustrated
by Robert Sauber.
p. cm. (Her story)
Summary: Unable to endure discrimination in his small Mississippi
town when he returns home from serving in France during World
War I, Flo's father moves the family to Chicago, where jazz symbolizes
the freedom he hopes they will find.
[1. Afro-Americans–Fiction. 2. Family life–Illinois–Chicago–Fiction.
3. Chicago (Ill.)–Fiction.] I. Hoobler, Thomas. II. Sauber, Robert, ill.
III. Carey-Greenberg Associates. IV. Title.
PZ7.H76227F   1997
[Fic]–dc 20   96-31785   CIP   AC

Table of Contents

Chapter 1
Homecoming

The day Daddy came home from the Great War, Flo was hoeing weeds. She promised Momma that she'd finish the job before going down to the road to wait for him.

It was February 1919. The war had been over for months. At first, Flo and her little brothers had run down to the road from Parkersville ten or twelve times a day to see if Daddy was coming home.

Momma said there wasn't any point in doing that. "He's way off across the ocean in France," Momma told them. "It'll take a while for the army to send all the soldiers back. And your Daddy will likely be on the last boat."

"Why's that?" asked Bubber, who was only four. He didn't understand about such things yet.

"Because he will," Momma replied.

But Toby, five years older than Bubber, told him

the real reason. "Negroes always are at the end of the line. Daddy will have to wait till all the white soldiers have gone home first."

Momma got angry when he said that, but Flo knew it was probably true. It didn't make waiting any easier. Daddy had been gone nearly two years, and they worried every single day that he might be killed.

Once a month, they would get a letter from him. He sent them most of his army pay, and wrote to tell them he was safe. Momma put all the letters in a drawer and sometimes took them out to read at night.

In one letter, he'd sent a picture of himself in his army uniform, and Momma tacked it on the wall. Flo looked at it every day and said a prayer that he'd be home soon.

That day, hoeing the turnip patch, Flo had gotten angry. She was tired of going down to the road. It was hard to sit there every day waiting and never seeing Daddy. She took it out on the weeds, hacking at them with all her strength. "Come home," she said as she dug up each weed. "Come home... come home."

And then she heard him laughing. At first she thought it was her imagination. But when she looked up, there he was. Just like the photograph, in his uniform. With a khaki cap and boots tightly laced up, and shiny brass buttons up the front of his jacket.

"Is that my big girl Florence?" he called to her,

holding his arms open wide.

Flo screamed and dropped the hoe. She ran over, and he picked her up and twirled her around, just like always.

In half a second, everybody else was there too. Momma and the boys grabbed Daddy, shouting and laughing and crying all at once.

"I'll bet you're hungry," Momma said at last, wondering when he had eaten last.

"Well, I walked from Vicksburg," Daddy said. "Got off the train there this morning. A porter gave me a sandwich, but I haven't eaten since then."

3

"From Vicksburg!" Momma said. "That's almost fourteen miles!"

"One thing about the army," Daddy said. "It gets you used to walking."

"We didn't know when you'd be here," said Momma. She turned to Flo. "Take fifty cents from my purse and go into town to buy a chicken."

"That's too much money," Daddy said.

"Prices have gone up," Momma told him. "But I've saved a lot from your pay. And Toby, you run on over to Aunt Lil's and tell her your Daddy's back. Invite her to dinner. We're going to celebrate."

It wasn't far to Parkersville, but Flo had to wait a long time at the store. White customers kept coming in, and Mr. Beauchamp tended to them first. Flo hopped back and forth from one foot to the other.

Finally, Mr. Beauchamp turned to her. "A nice large chicken, please," she said. She put the fifty cents down on the counter.

"You seem to be in a mighty big hurry," Mr. Beauchamp said.

"My daddy's come home," she told him.

He peered at her. "Your daddy?" he said. "Which one's that?"

"Bill Robinson."

"Oh, Big Billy's back from the war, is he?" said Mr. Beauchamp. "Ed Tuckman'll be glad to hear

4

that." Flo didn't like the way he smiled, but she just nodded politely.

Before the war, Daddy had sharecropped for Mr. Tuckman. He planted and tended a crop on Mr. Tuckman's land. At harvest time, Mr. Tuckman sold the crop and gave Daddy part of the money, keeping the rest.

Daddy made a lot of money for Mr. Tuckman that way. So when Daddy signed up for the army, Mr. Tuckman had tried to keep him from going. But Daddy went anyway.

One day Flo had heard Mr. Tuckman complaining to some other white men. "It's a shame that the army is so bad off that it took my best Negro," he'd said. It made her angry. Daddy isn't your Negro, she thought. Slavery's been over for fifty years. Every January 1, when most people celebrated New Year's, Daddy had told them this was the day Lincoln had freed the slaves in 1863.

By the time Flo got back home with the chicken, some of their friends had come by. Word traveled fast that Daddy was back. Some people had brought jars of preserves and covered dishes of food.

As Flo watched Daddy talking and laughing, she realized that he had changed. Or maybe she just didn't remember him so well. He was still full of fun and smiles. But there was something new inside of him. It made him look even stronger than she'd remembered.

Others noticed it too. "You look remarkably good, Bill," said one of his friends. "Did you ever get shot at in the war?"

Daddy's face turned serious. "I did. Let me tell you, that makes you think."

"I guess it would." Everybody laughed, except Daddy.

He leaned forward. "Made me think if I was good enough to fight for my country, I shouldn't take second place to any man at home."

Everybody fell silent. Flo heard a chair scrape on the floor. Daddy looked so fierce that people kind of moved away from him.

"You know," Daddy went on, "those people in France didn't care what color I was. They were mighty glad we came over to fight the Germans. One family invited me to dinner."

"You mean a white family?"

"All the French are white. But that family treated me just like I was their kin. Made me the best dinner I ate all the time I been gone. They had a piano, so I sat down and played them some songs."

"Oh, well, that explains it." People laughed again, but not so loud this time.

"No, it don't," said Daddy. "I knew they thought

I was just as good as they was. And I wondered why that should be any different when I went home."

Flo saw people start to look at each other. "Well, Bill," somebody said, "this is Mississippi, not France."

"This is the United States of America," Daddy said. "And we are part of it. What do you think would happen if we said we wouldn't work unless we got more of the crop? Or if we had a school for our children as good as the white school?"

Flo saw heads shaking all over the room. "Bill, you know what would happen."

Daddy folded his arms. "I don't know, because we never tried it."

Just then the door opened and in came Toby with Aunt Lil. "Oh!" she cried in her soft little voice. "God heard my prayers, and you've come back."

Daddy stood up to hug her. She was so tiny that she almost disappeared in his arms. "Let me see your hands," she said. Daddy let her go and held out his big hands. Flo had never seen anybody else with hands like Daddy's. His long fingers widened out at the tips, just like spoons.

Aunt Lil had raised Daddy after his parents had died when he was young. She had taught him to play the piano at the Negro Baptist Church. She turned his hands over to look at them. "God's gift," she said. "Do your hands still have the gift?"

"I can tell you about a French family who thought so," he said. "But right now, let's sit down and eat. Will all the rest of you stay too?"

But somehow, everybody else found an excuse not to stay. When they'd gone, Aunt Lil said, "That's strange. I knew they wanted to see you almost as bad as I did. Why'd they leave like that?"

Daddy shrugged. "Guess they had someplace else to go."

Flo knew the real reason. She'd seen it in their friends' faces when they left. Daddy had scared them.

Chapter 2
Sunday Meeting

Next morning was Sunday, and the Robinsons dressed in their best clothes for church. It was the only day of the week that the children wore shoes. Flo was wearing a new blue dress that Momma had made for her, and she felt grown-up.

The church was just a little wooden building with a cross on top. Daddy's daddy had helped build it years before, after the slaves were freed. When the Robinsons came inside, Reverend James beckoned Daddy to come forward. They shook hands warmly.

"Welcome home, Brother Robinson," Reverend James said. "We prayed for your deliverance from the field of battle."

"I felt the Lord with me," Daddy said. He winked. " 'Course I kept my head down when the bullets flew over."

Reverend James laughed and clapped him on the

back. "Will you honor us by playing the piano at the service?"

"I thought about that piano all the time I was gone," said Daddy. "I can't wait to feel those keys again."

"Your daughter took your place while you were gone," Reverend James said with a nod to Flo.

"Aunt Lil taught me," Flo told Daddy. "But I can't play anything like you can. Everybody wants to hear you, Daddy."

Flo took a seat in the choir while Momma and the boys sat down with the rest of the congregation. Daddy came over and spoke to Aunt Lil, who led the choir.

Daddy had always played "Roll, Jordan, Roll" to begin the service. The lively song had put people in a joyous mood.

But this time he picked something different. Aunt Lil looked a little nervous as she passed out the songbooks. They only had four books, so the choir had to share them. "Page 24," Aunt Lil whispered. "We haven't practiced this song, so do your best."

Reverend James stood up and led everybody in a prayer of thanks for Daddy's return. "I'm sure we're all glad," he said, "to have Bill Robinson lead us in song again."

Daddy started playing almost at once. Flo knew

that some of the keys on that piano didn't work, but Daddy made it sound beautiful. He sang as he played. Flo joined in with the rest of the choir, trying to keep up with him:

You got a right,
I got a right,
We all got a right,
To the tree of life.
Yes, the tree of life.

Every time I thought I was lost,
The dungeon shook
And the chains fell off.
'Cause God in the heaven
Answered my prayer.

As the choir repeated the verses, Flo understood. Daddy was trying to tell people how the war had changed him.

Others knew it too. When the song was over, Reverend James started to speak about the tree of life. "We all want that tree to grow tall and strong," he said. "But some trees grow on rocky ground. Or in a desert place, where the rain does not fall. The tree struggles, as all of us do. But we must endure our suffering."

Daddy softly played the tune to "We All Got a Right," again. Reverend James glanced at him and lowered his head. "Let us pray now," he said, "that each of us finds a place to grow and bear fruit in the warmth of the Lord."

Then Daddy began to play another song. It began, "I'm a-rolling in an unfriendly world." Aunt Lil called out the number, and the pages of the song-books flapped as they tried to find it. Daddy's deep voice spread through the church as he sang, "Brothers, won't you help me? Sisters, won't you help me? To make our people free!"

The last words weren't in the songbook. Daddy had made them up himself. Flo could feel the silence in the church as his voice died away. She saw people nudging each other and whispering. Daddy had scared them again.

Someone called out, "Come on, Bill! Play 'Roll, Jordan, Roll!'"

Daddy turned away from the piano and looked out at his friends and neighbors. Flo saw him smile and nod his head. Then he began to play the song they wanted.

His fingers pounded the keys as if he were angry. He played the old familiar tune like he never had before. Even so, people were happy to hear it. Flo's heart soared as she sang the words. It seemed just like the old times, before Daddy had gone off to war.

Everybody in the church rose up from their seats and began to clap and sing along. They kept on repeating the verses, making Daddy play until everybody had enough.

When the service was over, Flo saw Reverend James go over and talk to Daddy. The reverend didn't look angry exactly. More like worried. He gave Daddy a newspaper.

As the Robinsons walked home, Momma remarked, "I never heard you play that way before, Bill."

"I always play what's in my heart," he said. Momma took Daddy's hand and squeezed it. Flo could see that Momma was telling him she understood. But she looked as worried as everybody else had.

Mr. Tuckman was waiting when they got back to their house. He had on his Sunday suit too, and Flo guessed he'd come from the white church.

"Big Billy," he said, smiling. "I guess you're glad to be back. You get through the war all right? Didn't get shot or anything?"

"I feel real good," Daddy said.

"Just in time too. Cotton has to be planted next month, you remember."

"Oh, I know that," Daddy said.

"I suppose you want to take forty acres just like always," said Mr. Tuckman. "Unless you think you can handle a few more acres, with your young 'uns old enough to help out now." He looked at Flo and Toby, kind of measuring them. Flo felt like a horse he was thinking of buying.

"Why don't you come inside, and we'll talk about it?" Daddy said.

Mr. Tuckman stared at him. Flo heard Momma take a deep breath. Mr. Tuckman had never been inside their house. He glanced at the doorway as if it led into someplace awful. Flo's face burned. Daddy shouldn't do this, she thought.

"We could offer you a glass of lemonade," Daddy said.

Mr. Tuckman's jaws worked back and forth as if he were chewing on something tough. Finally he said, "Well, I guess I can spare a minute." Flo knew then how badly he really wanted Daddy to sharecrop for him.

Inside, Mr. Tuckman looked around as if he were surprised to see they had chairs and tables. He didn't take off his hat though.

Momma hurried off to the kitchen, pushing the children ahead of her. "Oh, my goodness," she kept saying as she took the pitcher of lemonade from the icebox. "It's not even cold. We should have bought a block of ice yesterday."

Flo wished Momma would be quiet. She wanted to hear what Daddy and Mr. Tuckman were saying. "I'll take it out to them," Flo said when Momma had poured the lemonade.

"Me too," said Toby. He was as eager as Flo to see what was going on.

"No, just Flo," Momma said, catching hold of Toby's shoulder. "Remember your manners, Flo."

"Momma," Flo said, rolling her eyes. As if she didn't know that!

Mr. Tuckman was sitting on the edge of their best chair as if he were afraid there were pins in it. Flo curtsied and gave him one of the glasses of lemonade. He put it down on the table next to him.

When Flo gave Daddy the other glass, he winked at her. She looked back at Mr. Tuckman, who still had his hat on. "May I take your hat, Mr. Tuckman?" she said.

She almost wished she hadn't said it. But that was polite, wasn't it?

Mr. Tuckman reached up as if he hadn't realized he was wearing a hat. "No," he muttered. "I'm not staying long." But he took it off and put it on his lap.

"Go help your momma now, Florence," Daddy said. She walked back to the kitchen. Her heart was pounding as if she'd done something very daring.

Momma, Flo, and Toby all pressed their ears to the kitchen door to hear what was being said. At first the two men talked quietly, but gradually Mr. Tuckman's voice rose.

"Things haven't changed down here, Big Billy," Mr. Tuckman said. "Nobody will hire you except me."

"That may be true," Daddy said. "But I believe it's fair for you to give me more of the crop. Prices have gone up."

"I'll worry about prices," Mr. Tuckman said. "I know all about them. Your job is to get as much cotton grown and picked as you can. If you grow more, you'll get more. Those kids can help you now. But your share will stay the same."

Daddy said something they couldn't hear in the kitchen. Whatever it was, it made Mr. Tuckman angry. "You've heard my final offer," he shouted. "And in two weeks, I want to see you start planting!"

Right after that, the front door slammed. Flo looked at Momma. She was shaking her head and saying, "Oh, my goodness," again.

Toby looked at Flo. His eyes were big. "Are we in trouble?" he asked.

Flo bit her lip. She didn't know what to tell him.

The kitchen door opened, and Daddy came through, carrying the glasses. One of them was still full. "Mr. Tuckman didn't seem to want any lemonade," he said.

Momma put her arms around him. "Oh, Bill, please be careful," she said.

"I will," he told her.

Chapter 3
The Burning Cross

Momma shooed the children outside to play. Flo suspected she wanted to talk to Daddy alone. But when they came back, Daddy was sitting in his favorite chair reading the newspaper Reverend James had given him.

Daddy had always loved to read, but this newspaper seemed particularly interesting to him. Even when Momma put supper on the table, Daddy brought it with him. Momma gave him a look, and he finally put it aside.

"What's in that newspaper?" Flo asked.

"News about us," Daddy said.

"About us?" Flo was puzzled. "Who would write anything about us?"

Daddy smiled. "It's all about the people of color in the United States. It's owned by a Negro, written by Negroes, and meant to be read by Negroes."

Toby looked skeptical. "Daddy, you're joking with us," he said.

"No," Daddy said. "It's called the *Chicago Defender*. You know where Chicago is, Toby?"

"Way up North somewhere," Toby said.

"It's in Illinois," Flo said. She had spent a lot of time looking at the geography book in their school. She loved maps.

Daddy was pleased. "These are sharp children we've got, Amelia," he told Momma.

"Yes, but they need clothes and shoes and food too," Momma said. "And reading newspapers don't earn money."

Flo was surprised. She couldn't remember Momma ever speaking to Daddy that way before the war. Momma must be very upset about the argument Daddy had with Mr. Tuckman.

Daddy was quiet awhile. Then he said, "This newspaper says Negroes are earning a lot of money in Chicago. Factory jobs there pay six dollars a week."

Momma dropped her fork. Daddy grinned at her. "That's $300 a year. Best year I ever had as a sharecropper, I got $90 as my share."

"Just because it says so in that newspaper don't mean it's true," Momma said.

After supper it was too dark to read inside the house. They had oil lamps, but didn't use them much because oil was expensive. Daddy went out on the porch with his newspaper.

Flo followed him. He read until the stars began to come out. When he finally put the newspaper down, Flo said, "Do you want to go to Chicago, Daddy?"

"Would you like that, Flo?"

"I don't think so," she replied. "We don't know anybody there. All our friends are here."

"Your Momma wouldn't either," he said. "So I'll go into town tomorrow and see if I can find work."

Next day, Flo and Toby walked to school as usual. It was only open in the winter, because all the children worked in the fields the rest of the year.

The school had only one room, and Reverend James's wife was the teacher. She put all the younger children in front of the chalkboard and began to teach them to add sums. Flo knew all that already, so she asked to look at the geography book.

She opened it to the map of the United States. Chicago wasn't hard to find. It was on the edge of a big lake. Lake Michigan. Flo stared at it. It was almost half the size of the whole state of Mississippi. She tried to imagine what a lake that big would be like.

Parkersville was too small a town to be on the map, but Flo found Vicksburg. She traced her finger up the Mississippi River from there. Almost a thousand miles, she figured. Chicago wasn't on the river.

You'd have to ride a train to get there from here, she thought. It'd be a long trip.

On the way home from school, Toby asked Flo, "Do you think Daddy would really take us to Chicago?"

"I don't know," she replied. "I think he'd rather stay here."

"But he'd have to work for Mr. Tuckman again," Toby said.

"Maybe he'll find a job with somebody else," said Flo.

"Naw," Toby told her. "White folks all stick together. You remember last year when Lucas Brown went away to the next county? The sheriff brought him back and made him work for Mr. Tuckman."

"That's because Lucas owed Mr. Tuckman money. Daddy doesn't owe anybody money, I don't think."

"They'd find some way," Toby said. "The whites still think they own us."

When Daddy came home, he looked discouraged. "Almost had a job," he said to Momma. "I went to George Jones's stable and told him that he ought to get into the business of fixing automobiles."

"Nobody around here owns one of them things," Momma said.

"They will soon," said Daddy. "I drove a truck in the army. It went faster than any horse could, and never got tired. I think George Jones believed me. But he just shook his head and said I'd have to get Mr. Tuckman's permission."

Daddy was stubborn. In the next few days, he went to just about everybody he could think of to find work, even to another white farmer, Mr. Younger. "He threw me off the place before I opened my mouth," Daddy told them. "Called me a trouble-maker and said I was lucky Ed Tuckman didn't take a whip to me."

Word got around that Daddy wouldn't give in. And just like Toby had said, the whites turned against them. One day Flo went to Mr. Beauchamp's store to buy some potatoes. He paid her no mind, even though nobody else was in the store. When she put a dime down and asked for potatoes, he just pushed it back. "Your money's no good here," he said. "Tell your daddy folks are going to teach him a lesson."

Flo came home and told Momma, who looked a lot more worried than Flo expected. "It's all right, Momma," Flo said. "We can eat turnips instead of potatoes. Maybe we could raise chickens."

"Child, it's not the food," Momma said. "You don't know what kinds of terrible things can happen."

That very night, after they'd all gone to bed, Flo woke up. She thought she was having a bad dream. Somebody was yelling in their front yard. Toby jumped out of his bed, and Bubber began to cry.

Momma ran into their room and took the children in her arms. "Be quiet," she whispered.

"What's wrong, Momma?" Flo asked.

"It's nightriders," Momma whispered. "The Klan."

Flo shivered. She'd heard about the Ku Klux Klan. Children at school said they took Negroes and whipped them, burned them… hanged them from trees. But the stories were always about people miles away. Not anybody she knew.

Sounds like hammering came from the front of the house. Then Flo heard glass breaking. The nightriders were throwing rocks at their house.

"Where's Daddy?" Toby asked.

"I told him to hide under our bed," said Momma. "But he's too proud."

Flo slipped out of Momma's arms and ran out of the bedroom. She heard Toby's footsteps behind her.

The house was completely dark, but when they reached the front room they could see Daddy. The nightriders were carrying torches, and firelight shone through the broken windows. Daddy was standing near a window, watching them.

Flo and Toby wrapped their arms around him. Flo could feel him shaking, but his fists were clenched tight. She knew he wasn't afraid—just angrier than she'd ever seen him.

"Run out the back, Daddy," said Toby.

"Get away," Flo said. "Don't let them kill you."

"They won't kill me," he said.

"There's too many of them, Daddy," said Flo. "You can't fight them all."

Suddenly, the room grew brighter. Something bigger than torches had started to burn outside. Flo and Toby drew back from the window. "They're going to burn our house!" Toby said.

"No," Daddy told him. "Come over and look."

They peered out the window nervously. A cross as high as their house was aflame, lighting up the whole yard. All around it were people wearing white sheets and masks.

"You see, they hide their faces," said Daddy. "They're cowards, really. But see that gray horse? Whose horse is that?"

Flo recognized it. "Mr. Tuckman's," she said.

"Yes, and the reddish one with a white star on its forehead?"

"I've seen Mr. Younger riding it in town," Toby said.

"Yes. That's all they are. People we know. Mr. Tuckman doesn't want to kill me, because then I can't work. He just wants to scare me."

"They'll kill you if you make them." That was Momma's voice, behind them. She had come out in the front room. "If you don't work for him, they have to kill you to show that a Negro can't beat them."

"There's another way, Amelia," Daddy told her.

That was when Flo knew they were going to Chicago after all.

Chapter 4
"We're on Our Way!"

Daddy went first. "It's better if I go ahead to find a job and a place for us to stay," he told them. "And it's safer for you if I travel alone."

"Why is that?" asked Flo. After the cross-burning she couldn't wait to get out of Parkersville.

"Mr. Tuckman might try to stop me," Daddy said. "They've done that in other places, forced Negroes off trains or riverboats. They want them to stay and work."

Late one night Reverend James drove up to their house in his wagon. Daddy hugged them all. "I'll be all right," he said. "And pretty soon we'll be together again."

"They're going to Jackson," Momma told the children after he'd left. "Nobody knows your daddy there, and he can catch a train for Chicago."

Daddy was right to be careful. Mr. Tuckman was

madder than ever when he found out Daddy was gone. He kept riding by on his horse, hoping to catch Daddy working outside. Then Momma told him that Daddy had just run off. "I don't know where he is now," she said.

Which was true. They didn't hear from him for weeks. Flo traced the route of the railroad on the map in the geography book, wondering which town Daddy had gotten to.

One day Reverend James brought them a letter. Daddy had sent it to him because he was afraid the post office would tell Mr. Tuckman if a letter came to Momma.

"Dear loved ones," she read. "I am safe and sound in Chicago. It's very different from Parkersville. But the *Defender* was right. Negroes can live in freedom here, just like anyone else.

"For now, I'm staying in a church basement. Reverend James knows the minister here. There are lots of jobs available, and I know I'll have one soon. As soon as I can, I'll send money for your train tickets. You are always in my thoughts.

"Love, your husband and daddy," Momma finished. She put the letter down and began to cry.

"Momma," said Flo, "it's all right. Daddy's safe and pretty soon we'll be with him."

"I know, I know," Momma said, wiping her eyes. "It's just that...I wish things could have worked out different. I'm afraid of Chicago."

"Why, Momma?" Toby asked. "It's got to be better than this place."

"I'm used to Parkersville," Momma said. "I've always lived here. Cities are big and dirty and strange. A lot of bad things happen there too. Only you don't know what to watch out for."

Toby and Flo thought she was worrying too much. In Parkersville, the white shopkeepers still wouldn't sell to the Robinsons. Mrs. James did the shopping for them. Every week Momma gave her some of the money she'd been able to save from Daddy's army pay.

Some of their neighbors brought them food too. It made Momma upset. "We never had to rely on people's charity before," she said.

"They just feel guilty because they wouldn't stand behind Daddy," Toby said. "They know they aren't as brave as him."

"Hush your mouth," Momma said. "They're kind folks. If I had to choose between kind and brave, I'll take kind any day."

One day, Reverend James came by. He looked worried. Right away Flo thought, Something's happened to Daddy.

The news was almost as bad. Reverend James had just received his weekly copy of the *Defender*. It said there had been a race riot in Chicago.

"Oh, my goodness," Momma said. "I knew it wasn't right for him to go there."

"What's a race riot?" Flo asked.

"There was fighting between Negroes and whites in Chicago," Reverend James told her. "People were killed."

Momma screamed. "Don't tell me!" she said. "Don't tell me Bill is dead!"

"I don't think he is," Reverend James said. "The *Defender* has a list of people who were injured, and he's not on it."

For the next two days, Momma prayed just the way she had when Daddy was in the army. Then Reverend James brought them a letter.

Daddy wasn't hurt. In fact, he was proud. "The Negroes fought back when white hooligans came into our neighborhood," he wrote. "We drove them out.

That could never happen in Mississippi. Here in Chicago a man can defend his home, no matter what color he is."

Momma shook her head. "Doesn't that sound just like him?" she asked. Flo remembered the burning cross. She knew how badly Daddy had wanted to fight back that night.

"I have good news too," Daddy's letter went on. "I found a job in a garage. They were looking for somebody who knew about cars, and that was me. So get ready to leave Parkersville. Soon I'll send you train tickets. And I have another surprise, but you'll see what it is when you get here."

"Hoorah!" Toby cheered. "We're getting out of this place at last."

Momma only worried more. Hearing about the riot didn't change her mind about Chicago. "What are we going to do?" she kept asking Flo. "We can't move our furniture. I don't even have a suitcase to pack our clothes in! Your daddy doesn't think about those things."

Their friends helped. Aunt Lil gave Momma an old trunk. Reverend James said he'd try to sell their house and furniture and send them the money.

"Wait a while," Momma told him. "We might come back."

Flo didn't think so. She was nervous about going

to Chicago too. But she knew that Daddy would never come back to work for Mr. Tuckman.

When the next letter came, Momma was afraid to open it. She knew by the way it felt that tickets were inside. But once she held them in her hand, she said, "We have to put our trust in God."

So early one morning before the sun was up, Reverend James brought his wagon to their house. Momma had been up half the night making food to take on the trip. They knew that the dining cars on the train would serve only white people.

They lifted the trunk onto the wagon, and started off. Flo turned back to look at their house one last time. It was the only home she'd ever known. She remembered the happy times her family had there. The garden that Momma had been so proud of. The stories that Daddy had told before the children went to sleep. Flo wondered if they would have as good times as those in Chicago.

At the train station, they had to wait outside on the platform. The waiting room was for whites only. When Bubber had to go to the bathroom, Toby took him around to the smelly outhouse with the sign, "For Coloreds." Everything they saw reminded Flo why Daddy wanted to move North. But would things really be any different there?

A whistle blew, and they looked down the tracks.

"Here it comes!" shouted Toby. Flo had seen trains go by on the tracks near Parkersville, but she had never been so close to one. As the engine stopped, a jet of steam blew out onto the tracks. They all screamed and jumped back.

A black man wearing a spotless white uniform and a red cap stepped down from one of the cars. He gave them a glance, and pointed to the rear of the train. "Last car," he said.

Toby and Flo dragged their trunk down to the end of the platform. Momma followed, carrying Bubber because she was afraid he'd fall onto the tracks.

They had trouble lifting the trunk up the metal steps of the car. Momma took Bubber inside and came back to help. At last the black man in the red cap came back and pushed it into the car. "Let me see your tickets," he said to Momma.

She took them out of her purse and handed them to him. He punched a hole in each one and gave them back. "Sit down and don't you get off this train unless I tell you," he said.

There were only a few other people in the car, and the Robinsons sat down by a window. The seats were hard wooden benches, and Flo wondered how long the trip would take.

With a lurch, the train started forward. Momma held tight to the siderail of the bench, but the children crowded around the window.

As they moved out of the station, the train began to pick up speed. Flo could hear the wheels of the car going clickety-clack underneath. She was moving faster than she ever had before.

"We're on our way, Momma," she said.

"Praise God," Momma said quietly. Her eyes were closed.

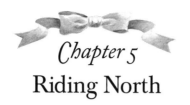

Chapter 5
Riding North

The trip was like having the geography book come to life. The Mississippi River ran along the train tracks, and Flo watched a line of barges headed downriver. In the distance a farmer plowed his fields. Three children riding a horse waved at Flo. A woman chased a dog away from her laundry hanging out to dry. In a second, they were all far behind. If you blinked, you missed something, Flo thought.

The train stopped every few miles to take on more passengers. When the man in the red cap came to punch tickets, Flo asked him how long it would take to get to Chicago. "Three days," he said.

That was why Momma had packed so much food. The boys were hungry already, but she made them wait to eat until the sun was high in the sky. By then, the car had heated up. Even though people opened the windows, everybody was perspiring and sticky and uncomfortable.

Momma gave them some lemonade, but Bubber wanted more. "You can't have any now," Momma said. "We have to make it last." Bubber began to whimper.

Flo tried to distract him by pointing out the window. "Let's see who can be the first one to spot something new," she said.

"Like what?" he asked.

"I don't know. Whatever we've never seen before."

"I never saw any of this before," Bubber said. "I want to go home now."

"Look at that!" Toby said. A shiny green cart was rolling down the road. But there wasn't any horse in front of it.

"That must be an automobile," Flo said. "Look how fast it's going. It almost keeps up with the train."

"Flo," Toby said, "do you think that's what the surprise is?"

"What do you mean?"

"In Daddy's letter, he said he had a surprise for us. You think he might have bought an automobile?"

Somebody in the seat behind them chuckled, and they turned around. A man sitting there said, "Your daddy had better be mighty rich to own one of them fool things."

"Well, he knows how to fix them, anyway," said Flo proudly.

In the middle of the afternoon, the man in the red cap brought two buckets of water and set them down in the car. People left their seats and drank from the dipper in each one. Bubber felt a little better after that. Momma soaked a handkerchief in the water, and they used it to wipe their faces.

Later on, she gave them some bacon, lettuce, and tomato sandwiches. At sunset, the train stopped at Greenville. That was one of the big towns mentioned in the geography book.

"I guess we'll stay here for the night," Toby told Flo. The man behind them laughed again.

"They're just taking on coal," he said. "This train don't stop till it gets to Chicago."

He was right. They were soon moving again. The man in the red cap hung up lanterns at each end of the car, and the passengers stretched out to sleep. People started to snore, but Flo kept listening to the clickety-clack of the wheels. It was spooky to look out the window and see the moon shining down. Everybody else in the world must be asleep, she thought, but we're moving just as fast as ever.

In the morning, they were all so stiff that they had to walk up and down the car. There was a smelly toilet in the back, but no place to wash themselves.

All the water in the buckets was gone, and Momma's lemonade was warm.

The most exciting thing they saw on the second day was Memphis. "We've left Mississippi," Flo said when the man in the red cap came by and announced that Memphis was the next stop. "We're in Tennessee now."

"It's big," Toby said as the train rolled into the city. Flo agreed. On the map, Memphis was just a dot, but it was the biggest place she'd ever seen. Some of the buildings were five or six stories high. Each one was right smack next to the other. Flo couldn't even imagine how people could stand to live in them. You wouldn't be able to breathe. Would Chicago be like this?

The train station was right in the middle of the city. As soon as the car stopped, a man got on board and began to sell sandwiches and drinks. When he saw Flo and the boys, he sang out, "Candy! I've got candy for the children! Only a penny."

Bubber pestered Momma so much that she gave them each a penny. Bubber picked out a red-and-white peppermint stick, and Toby chose a piece of twirled licorice. Flo bought a little bag of pretty red pieces, as small as ladybugs. When she put one in her mouth, though, she was surprised. "It tastes hot, like pepper!" she said. She put the rest in her pocket.

One of the new passengers took the seat right in front of theirs. Flo had never seen a Negro dressed like him. He wore a flat straw hat, a tight-fitting suit that was a beautiful tan color, and brown shoes that shone like mirrors. He carried a leather suitcase with a brass lock, and a strange-shaped black case.

The man smiled and tipped his hat to Momma, but she just nodded stiffly. Flo gave her a look of surprise. Momma was always friendly to just about everybody.

The train started on its way again. Flo kept staring at the back of the man in front of them. His hair was slicked down with something shiny, and the collar of his shirt looked as white and stiff as if it had just been painted.

Flo leaned closer. The man even smelled sweet. Momma tapped her arm and shook her head. She leaned over and whispered in Flo's ear, "Fancy man. Don't talk to him."

Flo didn't understand what Momma meant. But for the rest of the day, she looked out the window. Bubber kept asking when they could get off the train. He and Toby walked up and down the aisle, but there wasn't any place to go. It was still hot, and Flo's dress stuck to her. She wished she could take a bath.

That night, Flo kept waking up. She couldn't get comfortable at all. Every time she fell asleep, she had a dream about Chicago. Daddy was fighting a mob of white men who had set fire to their house. Only it was their house in Mississippi.

She woke up when the man in the red cap came into the car and shouted, "Cairo! We're coming into Cairo. You can move forward now."

Right away, the man ahead of them stood up. Carrying his suitcase and the strange black case, he walked through the door at the front of the car.

"Momma," said Flo. "He's going into the white section of the train."

"Well, they'll send him right back," Momma replied.

The man in the red cap heard her. "No, ma'am," he said. "We're in the North now. You can bring your children to the next car. The seats are more comfortable there. If you like, you can buy a meal in the dining car."

Momma refused to believe it. But when everybody else in the car left, Toby and Flo persuaded her to go too.

It was true. The seats in the next car were as soft as the easy chair in their house. And Toby soon reported that the toilet had a little sink where you could turn a knob to get water. Momma and Flo went back to see it for themselves.

Flo felt a lot better after splashing her face and

arms. She asked Momma if they could go to the dining car. "Oh, no, it'll cost too much," said Momma. "We still have enough to eat anyway."

"Just to look, Momma," begged Flo.

"Well, take the boys along and peek in and come right back," Momma said.

Flo's eyes opened wide when she saw the dining car. White tablecloths covered all the tables. China plates and silverware were set out on each table. And seated at the very first table was the man Momma had called Fancy.

He was cutting into a thick steak, and had mashed potatoes and green beans on his plate too. As he raised his fork, he saw them looking at him. He crooked his finger for them to come over. The boys went right up to him, but Flo followed slowly. She knew Momma would disapprove.

"First time you children been North?" he asked.

"Yessir," said Toby.

"Headed for Chicago, right?"

They nodded.

"You'll like it," he said. "It's the second-best city in the United States."

Flo was too curious to be silent. "What's the best?" she asked.

"New Orleans. But there's lots more money in Chicago. People spend money like it was water. I can

make as much in one week there than a month any-
place else."

"Do you fix cars?" Toby asked.

The man smiled and shook his head. "Nope. Just
blow on my licorice stick."

Flo and Toby exchanged glances. "We've got to
go back," Flo said. "Momma will start to worry."

"Want a piece of apple pie?" the man asked. "I'll
spring for one."

Flo grabbed Bubber's hand, because she knew
he'd say yes. "No, thank you," she said, pulling him
away from the table.

As they walked through the train, Toby said, "He
was joking with us, wasn't he?"

"I think so," Flo replied.

"'Cause I wondered if maybe I shouldn't have
eaten all my licorice," said Toby.

Chapter 6
A New Home

The seats in the new car were so soft that the children slept most of the afternoon. When they awoke, Momma gave them the last of the food. By the time they finished, it had started to get dark again. But through the window, they could see houses and stores with lights on inside.

"Is this Chicago?" Flo asked.

"I don't know," Momma told her.

"Look at that!" Toby cried. "Something's on fire!"

The sky was streaked with an orange glow. Plumes of smoke rose up from tall chimneys high above the ground. They came from a huge brick building that seemed almost as big as Parkersville. As the train sped by, the children saw a shower of sparks spurt out of one of the chimneys.

"It must be a factory of some kind," said Flo. She stared in wonder as it disappeared behind them.

She'd never seen anything like it before.

Soon, other factories just like it appeared. People in the car began to close the windows, because smoke was getting inside. Flo hoped this wasn't Chicago, because she couldn't understand how anybody could live here.

Then everything outside became completely black. The only light came from the lanterns inside the car. It's a tunnel, Flo thought. We're under the ground.

She told herself Chicago must be on the other side of the tunnel, but the train didn't even slow down. The tunnel went on and on, and she thought maybe they had taken a wrong turn. Then suddenly she felt the train's brakes come on. They were going to stop right here in the tunnel.

The man in the red cap came back and shouted, "Chicago! Illinois Central Station is just ahead. Make sure you take your belongings when you leave." He turned to Momma and said, "This is where you get off. Somebody meeting you here?"

"Yes," she said. "My husband."

"If you have any trouble, ask for the Urban League."

"How do we get out of the tunnel?" Flo asked.

The man chuckled, and she felt foolish. "There are steps that will take you upstairs," he said.

Flo and Toby carried the trunk while Momma held on to Bubber. As they stepped off the train, Momma gave a sigh of relief.

"There's only one thing could make me ever get on a train again," she said.

"What's that, Momma?" asked Flo.

"If it would take me back home to Mississippi."

There were dozens of people waiting out on the platform. Flo felt a sinking feeling in her stomach when she couldn't see Daddy in the crowd. What would they do if he didn't meet them?

He saw them first. When Flo heard him shout, she turned and saw him pushing through the crowd. He hugged Momma as the children swarmed around them. They were together again, Flo thought. Everything was all right now.

Daddy took them upstairs, and Flo stared. They were in the biggest room she'd ever seen. The ceiling was so high she could barely see it. The room was like one of those places where kings and queens lived—a palace! If this was where people in Chicago went to get on a train, what must their houses be like?

The first thing Bubber saw, though, was a place right in the middle of the big room. It was a store without any walls. All around it were stacks of newspapers, magazines, wrapped-up sandwiches, and more kinds of candy than anybody could imagine.

Bubber couldn't talk. He just pointed at the store and looked at Daddy.

"Want a treat?" Daddy asked.

"I already bought them candy on the train," Momma said.

"That was two days ago," said Toby.

"Did you get anything else to eat on the train?" asked Daddy.

"You don't think I'd let these children go hungry, do you?" replied Momma.

Daddy smiled and put his arm around Momma. "Well, let them have a little taste of Chicago, Amelia."

Momma threw up her hands. Daddy led them over to the store. A couple of white men were looking at the newspapers, but Daddy paid no attention to them. He scooped up some of the candy and paid for it. Neither of the white men seemed to mind a bit, Flo noticed.

That wasn't the only thing that was different about Chicago. Daddy took them outside and up some more stairs, which brought them to some more train tracks.

"Oh, no," said Momma. "Not another train."

"This is the El," Daddy told her. "We have to take it to get to the South Side."

"Don't you have an automobile?" Toby asked.

"What gave you that idea?" Daddy said.

"You said in your letter that you'd have a surprise for us."

"Well, when we get to the South Side, you'll see the surprise," Daddy said.

When the El train came, its doors opened right away, and Daddy pushed them inside. Good thing too, for the doors closed just as fast.

Flo couldn't believe it when Daddy found them seats right next to some white people. But nobody paid any attention when they sat down. Flo kept waiting for somebody to tell them to move to another car, but nobody did. Chicago sure wasn't like Mississippi, Flo thought.

It was fun to ride high above the ground. Lights stretched into the distance as far as Flo could see. There were buildings so high she didn't understand how they stood up. She couldn't believe how big Chicago was.

Even Momma was impressed. "Don't people here ever sleep?" she asked Daddy.

He laughed. "There's a lot more to do here than in Parkersville. Exciting things, Amelia. You'll see."

At last, Daddy told them the next stop was theirs. Momma stood up right away and dragged Bubber to the door. She'd seen how fast it opened and closed. Flo wondered if anybody ever got caught in it.

When they got off, the street was as bright as day.

People were walking along, talking and laughing. All the stores were still open. One of them had a huge sign of red and blue lights. Flo blinked as she read the word on the sign: "Palace."

"Is that really a palace?" she asked.

"It's a movie theater," Daddy told her. "We'll go and see a movie someday."

Daddy stopped in front of a high building. Flo leaned back to count the floors. Six! "This is our new home," Daddy said.

"Bill, this is too big for us," said Momma. "I'll never be able to keep it clean."

Daddy shook his head, smiling. "A lot of families live here. We just have one apartment."

Nobody understood what he meant till he took them inside and up three flights of stairs. I guess we'll have to get used to walking up stairs in Chicago, Flo thought.

There were doors all around them. Daddy opened one marked 3-E. They couldn't see anything, because it was dark.

"Now here's your surprise," Daddy said. He went into the dark room and all of a sudden a light went on. The room was filled with furniture.

"How'd you make that light go on?" Toby asked.

Momma didn't care. She headed straight for a chair and plopped herself down. Daddy showed the

children how to turn on the electric light by pulling a string from the ceiling. Everybody had to try it.

"Would you like to see the bedrooms?" Daddy asked.

The apartment was bigger than their whole house in Parkersville. Flo had her own room, with a soft bed and another electric light. When she turned on the light, she jumped to see a reflection of herself on the wall. It was a mirror, hanging on the door of a closet. Flo had never had a closet before, or a mirror either.

There was even a bathroom, just like the one on the train, only better. This one had a tub and faucets where both hot and cold water came out.

"We're rich!" Toby yelled after Daddy had showed them everything.

When Momma heard that, she looked suspiciously at Daddy. "How'd you get the money for all this?" she asked. "Just from fixing cars?"

Daddy put his arms around her. "Don't worry, Amelia. I didn't want to set you up in an empty apartment. I bought the furniture on time."

"What's that mean?" Momma asked.

"It just means we can have the furniture now, and all we have to do is pay a little bit every week to the store."

"Oh, my goodness," Momma said.

Chapter 7
A Visitor

The first thing Flo had to learn the next day was how to get around. There were so many streets, and they all looked alike. You could definitely get lost here, even if you never got on the El train.

Daddy pointed out that each street had a name or a number. They lived at 408 West Thirty-seventh Street. He made them repeat the address. "If you remember that," he said, "you can always find your way back."

Daddy took them to a restaurant for breakfast. It was called the Hattiesburg Diner, and the man who owned it was from Mississippi too. He served them bacon and eggs and grits just like Sundays back home. It put Momma in a good mood.

"Are we still in Chicago?" Flo asked Daddy when they went out on the street again.

"Sure are," Daddy said. "Why do you ask?"

Flo was a little embarrassed. "Well, when we came into the train station, there were lots of white people. But here there aren't any."

Daddy nodded. "This is the South Side of Chicago. Most of the Negroes live here. But that's good, because you see we have our own stores and restaurants and theaters. Everything we want."

"Where do the white people live?" Toby asked.

"Other places," replied Daddy. "If you walk two blocks that way, toward the lake, you'll come to Michigan Avenue. Don't go any farther than that, ever."

"Why not?" Flo asked. "I want to see the lake."

"We can go to the lake on the El," Daddy told her. "But if you walk across Michigan Avenue, you'll be in a white neighborhood. The kids there will chase you out."

It was confusing, thought Flo. You could ride on the El with white people, but you couldn't go into their neighborhood.

Momma asked Daddy to take them to a grocery store. She wanted to try out the gas stove in their apartment. He took them to a store that was a lot bigger than the one in Parkersville. Flo and Toby went up and down the aisles, looking at all the different kinds of food. But Momma almost left when she saw the prices. "Everything here costs so much," she whispered to Daddy. "Isn't there some other store?"

"The prices are the same all over," said Daddy. "That's just Chicago."

After they carried the groceries home, there was a knock at the door. Daddy nodded, and Flo opened it. A young woman with coffee-colored skin smiled at her. "I'm Lily Young from the Urban League," she said. "Is your mother home?"

Flo blinked. She remembered the man on the train telling them to go to the Urban League if they needed help. But she didn't know the Urban League came to you.

"Invite the lady in," Daddy said behind her. Flo opened the door wider to let her inside. Toby went to get Momma from the kitchen, and as soon as she saw the woman, she looked flustered.

Flo knew why. This woman was dressed better than anybody Flo had ever seen up close before. There wasn't a woman in Parkersville—black or white—who had a dress like hers. And her shoes had high heels! Momma was embarrassed because what she was wearing was a plain old green dress and floppy brown shoes. She never wore her Sunday clothes around the house.

"We're not ready to receive guests," Momma managed to say.

"I told the League when you'd arrive," Daddy

said. "Miss Young here can help you out better than I can."

Momma shot him a hard look, and Daddy suddenly decided to head for the kitchen. He pushed Toby and Bubber ahead of him, but Flo wanted to stay.

"Well, I guess you better sit down," Momma said.

Miss Young perched on the edge of a chair. Flo watched her carefully, and tried to sit just the same way—with her back straight and legs crossed at the ankles.

"I know it's going to be difficult for you to adjust to Chicago," Miss Young told Momma. "But that's what the Urban League is for—to help the migrants."

Migrants. Flo rolled the word around in her head. She knew immigrants were people who came from another country. Maybe she and Momma and Daddy were migrants, because Chicago seemed as strange as another country would be.

Miss Young went on talking. She told Momma how to do laundry, where you were supposed to put the garbage, and when to pay the bills for the gas and electric.

Momma kept nodding. Flo knew that everything Miss Young told her was helpful. But Momma hated to have some stranger come and tell her these things. It just reminded her that she'd left all her friends back in Mississippi.

Miss Young looked at Flo. "You'll want to make sure your children stay out of trouble," she told Momma.

"They're good children," Momma replied. "They never get in trouble."

Miss Young nodded. "Yes, but until school starts in September, they will need to find recreation."

Momma raised her eyebrows. Flo didn't know what that word meant either.

Miss Young saw they were puzzled. "Recreation means a way to occupy their time. They need exercise and opportunities for play."

"Well, I'll watch over them," Momma said.

"They can't stay here all day," said Miss Young. "And the streets can be dangerous for children."

Momma nodded. "Yes, I see that."

"I can come back tomorrow and take them to the YMCA."

"What's that?"

"A place where they can play. They can join sports teams, swim in the pool, take part in organized games."

"The pool?" said Flo.

"The Y has a swimming pool," said Miss Young.

Flo tried to imagine it, but couldn't. Somehow, she didn't think the YMCA was like the swimming hole in the woods where Toby and his friends went. "Do they have a pool for girls too?" she asked.

"Just one pool, but it's very large," said Miss Young.

"I wouldn't want to swim with the boys," Flo said. "I can't swim anyway," she admitted.

Miss Young smiled. "Boys and girls swim at separate times. And there will be an instructor to teach you."

Flo could see Momma wasn't quite convinced. "Does this cost a lot of money?" she asked.

"There's a small membership fee, but the League will pay it if you aren't able."

"I don't want to owe any more money," said Momma.

"It's twenty-five cents per year for each child," Miss Young said. "But for a dollar you can have a family membership. You could go too."

Momma laughed. "I don't need to play games," she said.

"The Y has singing groups, sewing circles, and evening classes for adults."

"Classes in what?"

"All sorts of things—cooking, embroidery, job skills."

"I got a job," Momma said. "Taking care of my family. But it looks like you want to do that for me."

"Many women hold jobs in Chicago," said Miss Young. "The migrants often find expenses here are higher than they expected."

"That I can well believe," said Momma. She finally told Miss Young she would talk it over with Daddy.

Miss Young gave her some papers to look at. "These will help you adjust to city life," she said.

As soon as Miss Young left, Momma gave Daddy what for. "Why didn't you tell me this woman was coming over?" she said. "I should have cleaned up the house and offered her something to eat. The woman didn't think I knew how to cook! She said I could learn at some place that would take care of my own children."

"The YMCA, Momma," Flo said.

"And they'd charge us money for it!"

Daddy already knew about the Y. He thought it was a good idea. "Don't worry about money so much," Daddy told Momma. "I'm making plenty of money."

When Flo mentioned the swimming pool, Toby got excited. Together, they wore Momma down, and she finally agreed they could join the Y.

"But I am not going, and that's final," Momma said. "That lady dropped a hint that I should have a job too. I'll bet she knew that all this furniture was bought on time."

"That's just the way things are done here," Daddy said. "Wait and see, Amelia. You're going to like Chicago."

Momma shook her head. "I'll never get used to it," she said.

Chapter 8
The Onion Club

The Wabash Street YMCA turned out to be the best place Flo had ever been to. She learned how to swim, and played games she never knew existed. Volleyball was her favorite. She made friends with a girl named Louise who lived in the building next to hers.

Toby and Bubber loved it too. Toby joined a basketball team, and on Saturdays the whole family went to watch him play. There was even a room for little kids where Bubber went. The woman in charge let them play with blocks and taught them games. At the end of the day, Flo and Toby could hardly get Bubber to go home.

Momma was lonely with Daddy at work and the children at the Y. She decided that the best way to make new friends was to join a church. Daddy had been going to one where hundreds of people came every Sunday. He liked it because it had organ music. But Momma said it was too big a church, and the minister wasn't like Reverend James.

She found another one along State Street. It was just a store, really, but a minister from the South had turned it into a church. It was small, but people crowded inside every Sunday and sang the old songs that they knew so well. Daddy wasn't so pleased, because the church didn't have an organ or a piano. Flo knew he missed playing the piano awfully bad.

Momma did make friends there—women just like her. All of them had moved North from the South too. When they came to visit, Flo could close her eyes and imagine she was back in Mississippi. But all everybody talked about was how terrible Chicago was. The high prices, the noise, the dirt. How bad the air smelled when the wind blew over from the meat-packing plants. All the places people could get into trouble.

The worst places of all, according to Momma's friends, were the jazz clubs. Jazz was some kind of music, as far as Flo could tell. People went to clubs all up and down State Street to hear it.

In fact, there was a jazz club they could see, located right across from their apartment. It had a big electric light outside that said "Onion Club." Momma just hated that! She wouldn't let the children go outside at night because of it.

But Flo and Toby would lean out the open window to watch the people going in and out. Wearing such clothes—oh my! Flo had never seen people with clothes like those. Except for Mr. Fancy on the train, and he couldn't hold a candle to some of the men going into the club.

And the women! Their clothes weren't trim and neat like Miss Young's. They were...well, Flo couldn't help but stare at the women and wonder what it would be like to dress like that. She giggled when she thought what Momma would say.

Strangest of all, Flo saw white men and women going into the club. She never saw white people on State Street in the daytime. But here they were. Jazz must be something everybody wanted to hear.

Many nights when Flo was supposed to be asleep, she lay awake listening to the music from the Onion Club. It was very different and new, just like

everything else in Chicago. She tried to imagine how to play it on the piano. Jazz had a secret about it that made her want to get up and dance.

Daddy thought so too. One Saturday evening while they were eating dinner, he said to Momma, "Why don't we go over to the Onion Club tonight?"

Momma almost dropped a platter of beans she was holding. "What did you say?" she asked him.

Hearing the tone in her voice, Daddy should have known better. But he went on anyway. "We could just stop in to hear the music," he said.

Momma took a deep breath. "Do you know what goes on in that club?"

"No, I never been inside," Daddy said.

"I should hope not," said Momma. "And I never will either!"

Daddy ate his food for a while, and then said, "Well, then, who wants to go to the lake tomorrow? After church, I mean."

The children cheered, and Daddy gave them a big wink. "Can't be as bad as the Onion Club, can it?" he said.

The day at the lake was the best time they'd ever had in Chicago. Maybe the best anywhere. When they got off the El at Jackson Park, the first thing Flo noticed was the air. It was so fresh and clean that it made her think of Mississippi.

They had to walk a few blocks, and then she saw the lake. It was even bigger than Flo had imagined. You couldn't see to the other side of it. Flo and the boys took off their shoes and stockings to run through the sand. When they got to the water, they just splashed right in.

Momma was annoyed that they'd gotten their clothes wet. She took them up to the tent where people changed into their bathing suits. Afterward, Flo and Toby showed off how they'd learned to swim at the Y.

"These children are going to need clothes for school more than bathing suits," said Momma.

"Aw, school," Toby said. "I wish we could just keep going to the Y every day."

"Two more weeks," Momma said.

Flo was a little nervous about school. Her friend Louise said white kids went there too. "Some of them call you names and stuff," Louise had told her. "But most of them aren't too bad."

Flo decided she wouldn't worry about that today. She was having too much fun. Even Momma finally took off her shoes and waded in the lake.

When a man walked by eating a long sausage on a roll, Bubber and Toby wanted one. Momma protested that she'd brought plenty of food for everyone. "It's a hot dog," Daddy said. "We'll just have to try one to see what it's like."

Momma stayed at their spot on the beach while Daddy and the children walked to the hot dog stand.

Of course, he bought five of them, along with cups of fizzy water that made your mouth feel sparkly when you drank it. Toby and Bubber ran ahead to give Momma her hot dog. Flo was glad to have a chance to talk to Daddy. "I wish Momma was happier about living in Chicago," she said.

"Well, now that she has friends, she'll start to feel more at home," he said.

"Did you ever hear this jazz music that she hates?" Flo asked.

"Once in a while," he said. "I sit out on the steps and listen to it from across the street."

"I can hear it in bed," Flo told him. "But I don't understand what's so bad about it."

"It's fast, for one thing," he said.

"I know," she replied. "I tried to think how to play it on the piano, but I couldn't."

"You hear it and think you know where it's going, and then it changes," Daddy said. "It takes a tune and turns it around. Looks for a new way to play it. Just like us, see. We're looking for a new way of life."

Flo didn't quite understand that. "It makes me feel like dancing."

He nodded. "Some of it does."

"Is that why Momma doesn't like it?"

Daddy thought for a while. "It's more because of the jazz clubs." He looked at Flo. "See, people get to drinking liquor and carrying on and doing things they shouldn't."

"What kinds of things?"

"Well, you better ask your momma about that."

Flo knew Momma wouldn't tell her.

"But don't you ever try to sneak into the Onion Club, hear me?" Daddy said with a smile.

Flo laughed. "Daddy, do you see what kinds of clothes the people wear in there? I haven't got any dresses like that."

That gave her an idea. "Do you suppose Momma would go to the club if you bought her some nice new clothes?"

"Well, I'll give it a try," he said.

Chapter 9
Names at School

Momma refused to buy any clothes for herself. "We've got to get these children ready for school," she told Daddy. "That's the one good thing about Chicago. Our children can get an education and make something of themselves. They're going to look just as good as anybody else."

So when Momma took Flo and Toby to the Moseley Elementary School, they had new clothes. Toby didn't like his blue knickers and high socks. They were scratchy, he said. But Flo was thrilled with her black patent-leather shoes and white stockings. That morning when she put them on, along with a new blouse and brown jumper, she looked at herself in the mirror. I wonder what they'd say if they could see me in Parkersville, she thought.

The school was a red brick building two stories high. "That can't be it," said Toby. "It's too big."

A teacher was waiting at the door, telling children which room to go to. She checked a list and couldn't find Flo or Toby's names. She told Momma they'd have to register at the principal's office.

As they walked in the direction she'd pointed, Toby whispered to Flo, "Maybe we'll be lucky and she'll send us home."

"Hush," Flo murmured, squeezing his hand. "Louise said they had a gym, just like the Y."

The principal was a white woman, tall and thin. She was scary just to look at. "I am Miss Underwood," she said, and Momma introduced herself.

"Is this your children's first time in school?" Miss Underwood asked.

"First time in Chicago," Momma said.

"I mean have they ever gone to school?"

"Oh, yes," Momma replied. "Their daddy and I made sure they went."

"Where was this?"

"Parkersville, Mississippi," said Momma.

Miss Underwood wrote that down and asked some more questions. Flo noticed she had a little gold watch pinned to the front of her dress. Flo was so fascinated by it that she didn't realize Miss Underwood had asked her what her name was.

Before she could answer, Miss Underwood said loudly, "Can you hear me?"

Flo looked up. "Oh, yes, ma'am."

"In the classroom, you must always pay attention when the teacher speaks."

Flo felt her face get hot. Miss Underwood put a piece of paper in front of her and handed her a pencil. "Write your name here."

Flo was nervous. She wasn't sure whether she was supposed to print or use what Mrs. James called cursive writing. She printed "FLO," because that seemed the quickest thing to do.

Miss Underwood looked at the paper. "You'll start in second grade," she said.

Second! Her friend Louise had said she would be in sixth grade. Flo hadn't been in a school with more than one room before, but she wanted to be with Louise.

Toby did even worse. When Miss Underwood asked him to write his name, he said, "I forgot how." Flo knew he was just saying that because he didn't like Miss Underwood.

Momma looked like she wanted to swat him. "You write your name down right now," she said in a voice that meant he'd better.

Toby scribbled his name, and Miss Underwood said, "First grade."

Flo was even more disappointed when she went to the second-grade room. Most of the other children were lots younger. At least she had her own desk. Back in her old school, the children sat on benches or the floor.

The teacher seemed a lot nicer than Miss Underwood, even though she was white too. "I am Mrs. Kaufman," she said. She wrote it on the chalkboard.

"Now let's learn what your names are," Mrs. Kaufman said. One by one, all the children said their names. Some of the white kids had names Flo hadn't heard before. Antonia, Sean, Christine, Jan... Chicago had all kinds of people.

Flo suddenly realized that Mrs. Kaufman was pointing at her. "Flo," she said, "would you like to help me pass out notebooks?"

Flo came up to the front of the room, and Mrs. Kaufman gave her some blue books. While Flo walked around giving one to each student, Mrs. Kaufman passed out thick black pencils.

She gave the last one to Flo. "You're going to be my helper this year," Miss Kaufman said. "Because you're the oldest."

Flo thought second grade might not be so bad after all. After Mrs. Kaufman explained that they could keep the pencils and notebooks, Flo was even happier. She'd never had her very own notebook before.

"Now the first thing I want you to write," said

Mrs. Kaufman, "is your names. I'll just come around to see how you're doing."

This time, Flo realized that writing her name was important. She opened the cover of the notebook. All the pages were blank. It was exciting to think that she was going to fill them up this year.

So she wrote her full name in cursive: Florence Robinson. When Mrs. Kaufman looked at her notebook, she seemed surprised.

"That's very good, Florence," she said. "Maybe you don't belong in second grade."

"Can I go to the sixth grade?" Flo asked.

"Well, not yet," replied Mrs. Kaufman. "I can only promote students to the third grade."

"I'd rather stay here till I'm ready for sixth grade," Flo told her.

As the day went on, though, Flo was bored. Everything Mrs. Kaufman taught, Flo already knew.

It was nice to have her own notebook and pencil, and later Mrs. Kaufman even gave out story books. Every student got one. When Flo opened hers, though, she found out that the stories were too easy to read.

Flo thought things would get more interesting when the class went to the gym. But they just did exercises instead of getting to play games.

After the bell rang at the end of the day, Mrs. Kaufman asked Flo to stay. Flo worried that she had done something wrong.

"I saw you looking through the reader," said Mrs. Kaufman.

"I guess I wasn't paying attention," said Flo. "I'm sorry."

"No, I understand," Mrs. Kaufman told her. "You can read everything in there already, can't you?"

"Yes, ma'am."

"Why were you sent to the second grade?"

Flo told her how she got nervous and printed her name for Miss Underwood.

Mrs. Kaufman nodded. "I think Miss Underwood made a mistake. But she won't like to admit that. I'll bring some other books for you to read tomorrow."

"Do you have a geography book?" Flo asked.

"We don't teach geography in second grade, but I can find one."

"I liked that best of all in my old school," Flo said. "Except we only had one book."

"Well, you'll have your own here, and I will give you special work to do. How's that?"

Flo felt proud. She went outside, looking for Toby. Momma had made them promise to walk home together.

At first she couldn't find him. But then she heard shouts, and turned to see a crowd of boys on the sidewalk. Flo walked over to see what was happening.

Right in the middle of the crowd, Toby was fighting some white boy. Flo pushed her way through and grabbed Toby. The other boy was still swinging his fists, but she shoved him away. He wasn't any bigger than Toby. "Aw, let 'em fight," a boy said. "It's an even match."

Toby's lip was bleeding, and his new clothes were all dirty. Flo shook him. "Momma is going to give you what for! How'd you get into a fight on the very first day of school?"

"He called me names," Toby explained. "Said I was dumb!"

The other boy ran after them. "Yah, yah, need your sister to save you," he shouted.

"See!" Toby said furiously. "I'll just have to fight him again tomorrow."

"Is he in your class?" Flo asked.

"Yeah, and we're both older than anybody else. Nobody even knows the alphabet! That principal sent me there because she thought I was dumb."

"But didn't you show the teacher that you knew how to read?"

Toby shook his head. "She wrote a big *A* on the board and asked if we knew what it was. I told her it was a *B*."

"Why on earth did you do that?"

"I don't know. I thought it was funny."

"So this boy said you were dumb."

"He's the dumb one. Somebody told me he had been in first grade last year. Didn't learn enough to go to second grade."

Flo sighed. "Toby, you have to show the teacher that you're smart. Then she'll move you to another grade."

"Yeah? Then I'd be in your grade. Did *you* get moved up?"

"No," Flo said. "But the teacher is real nice. She's going to give me special books."

Toby shook his head. "They just think we're dumb 'cause we're from Mississippi."

Chapter 10

The Victrola

Momma really lit into Toby when she saw his clothes. "Wait till your daddy gets home," she said. "He'll tan you good and proper."

But Daddy was late coming home. Of course that made Momma worry all the more. When he finally arrived, she forgot to tell him about Toby's fight.

"Bill!" said Momma when he came through the door. "Where've you been?"

He looked tired. "I found a second job," he said. "I met this man who needed somebody to drive a truck."

Daddy looked at Toby. "What happened to you?" he asked.

That reminded Momma. "He got into a fight the first day at school. With a white boy!" She waved Toby's dirty knickers, which she had been washing.

Daddy put his hand under Toby's chin. "That

so?" he asked. "Did you get any licks in?"

"I made his nose bleed," said Toby proudly.

"Bill!" Momma said.

"Mm-hm," said Daddy. "Well, Toby, you shouldn't start fights you don't have to. But you should defend yourself."

"Don't encourage him!" Momma said. "He isn't going to school for that."

Daddy nodded. He unrolled a copy of the *Defender* that he had under his arm. Now that they were in Chicago, he bought his own copy every week. "Look at this," he said, pointing to a headline.

It read: EDUCATION WILL FORCE OPEN THE DOOR TO SUCCESS.

"That's the truth," Daddy said. "Your momma and I didn't have the chance to go to a fine school. I learned how to fix cars in the army, though, so now I've got a job. You can do better than that."

"The principal put me in first grade," said Toby.

"Then that's where you start," said Daddy. "But you move up as fast as you can. If you study hard enough, you'll get to high school. There wasn't any high school for our race in Mississippi."

"They'll never ever let me get to high school," Toby said.

"Read this again," Daddy said, holding the newspaper under Toby's nose. "You don't worry what somebody will let you do. You force open that door."

He looked at Momma. "Isn't that right?" he asked.

"Well, it's your way of doing things, that's for sure," said Momma.

"Now how do I get my supper?" Daddy asked.

While Daddy ate, Momma cut out the article from the *Defender* and tacked it up on the wall. Flo looked through the rest of the newspaper. She read letters from people in the South who wanted to come North. It was true—everybody thought things were better up here.

She saw something else that interested her. The *Defender* was sponsoring a writing contest for children. It would give prizes for the best story explaining why your family came to Chicago.

I could do that, Flo thought. I'd tell about what happened when Daddy wouldn't work for Mr. Tuckman. Flo still got scared when she thought about the nightriders. And, she thought, I'll tell how Daddy got a good job and paid for our train tickets.

She started to work on it right away. The very first thing she wrote in her notebook was, "It began when Daddy came home from the war."

Momma had to tell her to turn out the light and go to bed. "Are you still doing homework?" she asked. "No, Momma," Flo said. She wanted to keep

the contest a secret for now. "We didn't have any homework."

"I didn't even get to ask you about your class," Momma said.

"It was fine, Momma. I like my teacher a lot."

"That's good. Flo, you know you got to look after your brother. I'm depending on you. Can you do that?"

Flo looked up. Momma sounded worried. "I'll try, Momma. Is there something the matter?"

Momma sat down on Flo's bed. "Your daddy is working so hard, that's all. I wish he hadn't taken another job. If Toby gets into trouble, I don't know what I'd do."

"He won't get into trouble, Momma," Flo said. "I'll make sure of it."

School started to get better after that. Toby took to heart what Daddy had told him. He showed the first-grade teacher that he knew how to read. The next week, she moved him up to second grade. So he and Flo were in the same class, and after school she kept him away from the boy he had fought with.

Mrs. Kaufman did bring a geography book for Flo. She also gave Flo some sheets of paper that were so thin you could see right through them. Mrs. Kaufman showed Flo how to put the paper over the pages in the geography book and trace the maps.

"Now you can test yourself," she told Flo. "Close the book after you've made a map and try to write in the names of the states and cities."

Mrs. Kaufman noticed that Flo was already writing in her notebook. "I hope it's all right to use it," said Flo. "I don't have anything else to write on."

"What are you writing?" asked Mrs. Kaufman.

Flo shyly explained about the contest. She let Mrs. Kaufman read the beginning of her story. "That's wonderful," she told Flo. "Keep it up, and if you need more paper I'll give you some."

"Do you think I'll win the contest?" Flo asked.

"It's hard to say," replied Mrs. Kaufman. "We don't know what the other entries will be like. Let me see it again when you've finished."

Momma was glad that Toby stopped fighting, but she was still worried about Daddy. He came home late every night now, sometimes after the children had gone to bed. The only day he didn't work was Sunday, and after church he slept most of the day.

One day Flo and Toby came home from school to find a big wooden box in the living room. "What's that, Momma?" they asked.

"I don't know," Momma said. "Your daddy bought it. All he told me was that some men were delivering something today."

"Can we open the lid and see what's inside?" Flo asked.

"Don't touch it," Momma said. She shook her head. "Whatever it is, you can be sure it cost money."

Daddy came home on time that night. He carried another package, wrapped in brown paper. Everybody rushed to ask him what was inside the mysterious wooden box.

"It's a Victrola," he said.

Toby looked at Flo. She laughed. "I don't know what it is either, Toby," she said.

Daddy opened the top of the box. Inside was a big black thing that looked like a horn. He connected it to the box, and then brought out a metal handle. That fit into a hole on the side of the box.

They kept asking him questions, but he just said, "Wait and see."

Finally he opened the package and took out a black plate with a hole in the middle. He put it inside the box. Then he started to turn the crank on the side.

All of a sudden piano music came out of the horn! They all jumped back. The box was playing "Roll, Jordan, Roll."

It was hard to believe. Momma just plopped down on the couch. Bubber kept trying to look inside the box to find out who was playing the music. "Is that a new kind of piano, Daddy?" Toby asked.

"No, but it'll play any kind of music you want," Daddy said. "These black things are called records. Each one has a song on it, and the machine plays it for you."

"But who's playing the piano?" Flo asked.

"The person who made the record is playing," Daddy told her.

"Could you make a record?" she asked. "I think you play the song better."

He laughed. "No, no, I don't think so."

"How much did this thing cost?" Momma asked.

"Not as much as a piano," Daddy said. "Don't worry, I paid for it by driving trucks."

"Does that mean you'll quit working nights?" Momma asked.

He gave her a little smile. "Well, I'd like to buy some more records."

Chapter 11
The Boarder

Flo finished her story for the contest. She decided that if she won, she would use the prize money to buy more records. Even Momma's friends liked to come over and listen to the Victrola. Flo had gotten tired of hearing them play "Roll, Jordan, Roll" over and over.

When Flo showed her story to Mrs. Kaufman, her teacher read it over quickly. "It's very good," she said. "Do you have the time to make another copy for me?"

"I have to mail it in tomorrow," Flo told her. "But I'll copy it tonight."

"I think there is something else I can use it for, even if you don't win the contest," said Mrs. Kaufman.

"Don't you think I'll win?" asked Flo.

"If I was the judge, you would," Mrs. Kaufman told her.

The next day, Flo went to the post office after school and mailed her story. On the way home, she decided not to tell Momma and Daddy about the contest just yet. Not till she won.

But that day, everything changed. When Flo got home, Momma wasn't there. Mrs. Williams, one of Momma's friends from church, opened the door and put her arms around Flo.

Flo knew right away that something was wrong. "Where's Momma?" she asked.

"She went to the hospital," Mrs. Williams said. "There's been an accident."

An accident. Flo felt cold all over. People said that when somebody got run over by a car in the street. Or when they burned themselves on the stove.

"Momma had an accident? How did it happen?" Flo asked.

"No. It's your daddy. He hurt himself at work. Somebody came and told your momma, and she asked me to look after Bubber."

Toby was home too. He tugged at Flo's sleeve. "Let's go to the hospital," he said.

"No," said Mrs. Williams. "It's too far, and they won't let children in. I told your momma that I would fix dinner for you."

It was hard to wait. None of them felt like eating. Mrs. Williams tried to cheer them up by telling about people she knew who had had accidents. "Pretty soon, most of them were fixed up as good as new. The doctors here are wonderful."

"Did Momma say what kind of accident Daddy was in?"

"No, she was in a hurry. Why don't we turn on the Victrola for a while to pass the time?"

Flo couldn't stand listening to the song. It reminded her too much of Daddy, how proud he'd been of the Victrola. *What if he can't work anymore?* she thought. *What will we do?*

Finally Flo told Mrs. Williams that she could go home. "We'll be all right," Flo promised.

"Well, if you need anything, my apartment is right downstairs," Mrs. Williams said.

Flo put Bubber to bed, and she and Toby sat on the couch. "Maybe Momma is just waiting for Daddy to get bandaged up," Toby said. "Then they'll come home together."

"Yes," Flo said. "Any minute now the door will open and they'll walk in. Daddy will laugh and show us how he got hurt."

"But he won't be hurt bad, will he?"

Flo shook her head. "No," she said. "Nothing can hurt Daddy. He got shot at in the war, remember."

"That's true," said Toby. "And it wouldn't be fair if he came up to Chicago and got... got himself... "

"Don't think that," Flo said. "Daddy couldn't be killed, not even in Chicago."

But they knew that wasn't true.

Both of them had fallen asleep when they heard the door open. Together, they jumped up. They saw Momma. Just her. Not Daddy.

"Is Daddy all right?" Flo asked.

Momma put her arms around them. "Oh, my babies," she said. "I told him he was working too hard."

"Tell us, Momma!" Flo shouted. "How's Daddy?"

Momma sat down. Flo could see she'd been crying. "He's in the hospital. His foot is all smashed. He was working on one of the cars, when something slipped and it fell on him."

"But he'll be all right, won't he?" Flo asked.

"I don't know," Momma said. "The doctor wouldn't tell me. Daddy has to stay in the hospital two or three days so he won't get blood poisoning. After that... he won't walk for some time. He can't work, that's for sure."

"Well, Momma, he will when his foot gets better."

"Who knows how long that'll be?" said Momma. "And we've got to pay the rent, the payments for this furniture, food, and I don't know what all." She put her head in her hands.

"I'll get a job!" Toby said. "I can sell newspapers on the street."

"You will not," Momma told him. "You're going right back to school tomorrow morning. I promised him you would. Now the both of you get to bed. There's nothing we can do tonight."

Flo couldn't sleep. She kept trying to think of ways they could make money. In the morning, she told Momma, "You remember that nice lady Miss Young? Why don't you go down to the Urban League and ask her what to do?"

Momma nodded. Flo could see she hadn't slept either. "I guess I could," she said. "I didn't like her, but she knows things. I'll go visit your daddy first."

After school, Flo and Toby ran home. Momma told them that Daddy was feeling better. "But he'll have to use crutches for at least two months. Till then, we have to make do."

Momma looked at Flo. "I went to see that Miss Young," she said. "She had two ideas, but we'd better get started. I don't think your Daddy will like either one of them."

"Toby and I will work if we have to," Flo said.

"No," Momma replied. "Miss Young said she could find me a job. Cleaning, mostly. Making beds and washing windows. If I'd taken a class, she said, I could cook."

"You can cook better than anybody, Momma," Toby said.

"Well, white folks in Chicago like different kinds of food, I guess."

"You're going to work for a white family?" Flo asked.

Momma nodded. "It won't bother me," she said. "Flo, you'll have to cook dinner here at home."

"I don't mind," Flo said.

"Then there's the other thing," Momma told her. "Do you think you could give up your bedroom and move in with your brothers?"

"We always shared the same room before," Flo said. "But what are you going to do with my room?"

Momma folded her hands. "Miss Young said we should take in a boarder."

"A boarder?" said Flo. "You mean somebody to live here?"

"Oh, Daddy won't like that, for sure," said Toby.

"Miss Young said she could find a boarder who would pay five dollars a week," Momma told them.

Toby whistled. "Of course," said Momma, "I told her I wanted somebody clean and respectable. She said she had a list of people that the League had approved."

They heard a knock at the door. Momma sighed and told Flo to answer it. "I said she might as well send somebody over today."

With Toby right behind her, Flo opened the door. A man stood there, dressed in a tight-fitting suit with a beautiful tan color. She blinked and tried to think where she'd seen that suit before.

"You're the fancy man from the train!" she said.

He looked at her. "My name is Claude Swallow," he said. "And I believe I remember you too."

Flo took him to meet Momma. She noticed that his clothes weren't so bright and clean as they had been. But he still carried the same leather suitcase and the strange-looking black case.

Momma showed Mr. Swallow the room, and he said, "This will be fine. I hope you won't mind if I practice my music during the day."

"Music?" said Flo. "Our daddy loves music."

Toby piped up. "You said you played a licorice stick. I want to see you do that."

Mr. Swallow smiled. "It's better known as a clarinet." He opened his black case, and they could see a long sort of flute with silver keys.

"What sort of music do you play on that?" Momma said suspiciously.

Mr. Swallow took the clarinet from its case and attached a mouthpiece. He put it to his lips and played a little trill. Flo liked the way it sounded, kind of high, like birds singing.

Then Mr. Swallow tapped his foot and began to play a song. They didn't recognize it, but Flo knew what kind of music it was. So did Momma. "That's jazz," she said as if she'd caught him stealing. "You're a jazz musician."

He looked at her and switched the tune around, making it slow and mournful, like funeral music. Flo giggled, and he winked at her as he put the clarinet down.

"Jazz is just music, ma'am," said Mr. Swallow. "Nothing bad about it. Whether or not it's good depends on who's playing it."

"There's no drinking allowed in my home," Momma said.

Mr. Swallow shook his head. "No, ma'am."

"No visitors."

"No, ma'am."

"Five dollars a week. In advance."

"Tell you what," said Mr. Swallow. "How about I give you six dollars, and you'll fix me one meal a day. I get up in the afternoon."

Momma thought about it. Flo nudged her. She knew how badly they needed the six dollars. "No noise at night," said Momma.

"No, ma'am."

Momma couldn't think of anything else. She threw up her hands. "A jazz musician," she muttered. "Oh, my goodness."

Chapter 12
Daddy Comes Home

Mr. Swallow kept his promises to Momma. She gave him a key so he could let himself in, and he went off to his job. After Flo went to bed, she lay awake for a while listening for him. But whatever time he came in that night, nobody heard a sound. When Flo woke up, the door to her old room was closed.

Momma told the children to be quiet getting ready for school, so they wouldn't disturb Mr. Swallow. "I'm supposed to start my job today," she said. "I'll leave Bubber with Mrs. Williams, and you can pick him up after school."

"Does Daddy know you've got a job?" Flo asked.

She shook her head. "I'll tell him when I visit the hospital after work. That means I won't be back till late. So you'll have to fix Mister Fancy Jazz breakfast or supper or whatever he wants. Just make sure he doesn't eat everything we've got in the kitchen."

"He's pretty thin, Momma," said Flo.

"The thin ones can fool you," Momma replied. "Look how much your brother Toby eats."

All day at school, Flo kept thinking about Mr. Swallow. She wanted to ask him what really went on in the jazz clubs. What was it like when all those beautiful women and handsome men came to listen to the music?

When she and Toby came home, however, Flo remembered to check the mailbox. Probably it was too early to expect a letter from the contest, but you couldn't tell. Maybe someone would read her story and decide it was the best they'd get.

There wasn't any letter. They picked up Bubber and went to their apartment. Flo smelled coffee, and when she went to the kitchen, there was Mr. Swallow. He was wearing the pants to his tan suit and a light blue shirt. She noticed that his suspenders had blue and yellow stripes. Mr. Fancy, she thought to herself with a smile.

"I hope you don't mind I made coffee," he said. "I can't start the day without it."

"Would you like anything else?" she asked. "I can fix fried eggs and toast some bread in the oven. We have a jar of grape jam."

"That sounds just fine," he said.

Flo fixed the eggs carefully and put them on a plate. He ate them up before she could toast the bread, and then gobbled that down too after spreading most of their jam on it. Momma was right. He sure seemed hungry.

"You have a spot on your shirt," she said.

He looked down and put his hand over it. Flo thought he seemed embarrassed. "I can wash it for you," she said.

"No," he said. "Just let me have a wet cloth."

She watched him dab the cloth on the shirt, but it didn't get all the spot out.

"Let me wash it," she said. "Momma has some good soap and an iron too."

He went back to his room and changed into another shirt, a white one. Flo saw why he didn't want to wear it. The cuffs were frayed, and it was almost gray from being worn so many times.

As she scrubbed the shirt in the sink, she said to him, "On the train, you said you could make a lot of money in Chicago."

"That's the truth," he said.

Flo hesitated, but couldn't keep from asking, "So how come you're not staying in a fancy hotel or someplace like that?"

He folded his arms and tilted the chair back. "You got sharp eyes, girl. I'll tell you the truth. I got into a card game and lost almost everything I made. Never play cards with a man named Doc."

"Oh, I wouldn't play cards with anybody," she said. "Not for money."

"That's a good policy," he said. "Stick to it."

While Flo heated the iron on the stove, Mr. Swallow said, "Your folks must be doing all right here. I see you got a Victrola. You think your momma would mind if I played it?"

"Please don't," Flo said. She laughed at the way he looked at her. "We only have one record," she explained. "And I can't stand to hear it any more."

"Just one record?" he said. "Why's that?"

"Daddy was going to buy more, but then he got hurt," she told him.

"Since you're taking care of my shirt," he said, "I'll see if I can scare up a couple more records."

"Momma doesn't like jazz," Flo told him.

"I think I figured that out," he said.

"But Daddy does."

"Well, let's just see what I can find."

After Flo finished ironing his shirt, Mr. Swallow went back to his room. She could hear him practicing on his clarinet. He was good, she decided. Maybe if she listened to him long enough, she'd figure out the secret of jazz.

He came out all dressed neat and clean again,

and said good-bye. "Don't wait up for me now," he said with a smile.

Flo fixed dinner for herself and the boys. She saved something for Momma, but when she got home, she had a big package of food. When she unwrapped it, Flo saw big pieces of chicken and some chocolate cake.

"Where'd all this food come from?" Flo asked.

"You can't imagine," Momma said. "Oh, my goodness."

Toby and Bubber started asking for some, even though they'd eaten only two hours earlier.

Momma cut pieces of the cake and gave it to them. "This is all from the house where I work. I knew there were rich people in this world, but I never saw any house like that. They have three other maids besides me, a cook, and some man who serves dinner. Cook let me have some of the leftovers, because the family doesn't like to eat the same thing two days in a row."

"What are they going to have tomorrow?" Toby asked with a gleam in his eye. He reached out for some of the chicken.

"Don't be so greedy," Flo told him. "Momma, did you visit Daddy?"

"Yes, I did, and he's hopping around on his foot like he wants to run home. But the doctor has told him he has to use a crutch."

"Will he be able to go back to his job?" asked Flo.

"He thinks so. He says he's coming home tomorrow. But he can't work with that foot."

"Did you tell him about the boarder?" Toby asked.

Momma nodded. "He didn't much like that, even when I said he was paying six dollars a week." She looked at Flo. "So I told him that Mr. Fancy was a jazz musician. Did he give you any trouble, Flo?"

"He was very polite, Momma. He likes coffee. I ironed his shirt for him, and he said he'd bring us some records for the Victrola."

"Well, your daddy will like that."

She was right. The next day when Flo and Toby came home from school, they could hear music coming from their apartment. Daddy and Mr. Swallow were playing records on the Victrola.

Flo and Toby ran to hug Daddy, and he got up from the couch with his arms open. Flo could see that it hurt him to stand. She looked at his foot. It was covered with hard plaster. A crutch lay on the floor, but Daddy didn't pick it up.

"Does it hurt?" Toby asked.

"Naw, it's fine," Daddy said. Flo made him sit down again. She knew he was too proud to let them see him use the crutch.

"Mr. Swallow tells me you cook pretty good," said Daddy. "How about making something for both of us? That hospital food was terrible."

Flo was glad to be doing something. As she fried eggs in the kitchen, she could hear the music playing in the living room. Mr. Swallow started to play his clarinet too.

When she came out with their plates, Daddy was talking to him about jazz. Daddy's hands were moving as though he were playing the piano. Toby and Bubber were hopping around the room. You couldn't help but like jazz, Flo thought. Except for Momma, but maybe she'd hear the records and change her mind.

"How long has it been since you played a piano?" Mr. Swallow asked Daddy after they finished eating.

He shook his head. "Too long. Wish I could get my hands across a keyboard again."

"I can't promise anything," said Mr. Swallow, "but the band I play for needs a piano man."

Flo could see Daddy's eyes flash from across the room. Her stomach fell when she thought what Momma would say.

"How far away is the club you work in?" Daddy asked.

"Only a couple blocks. But you don't have to go

today. Rest up a little."

"I been on my back for almost a week," Daddy said. "And I got here from the hospital by myself." He pushed himself to his feet.

Flo picked up his crutch and made him use it. "I only need this for a few days," Daddy said.

"I'll make sure he gets back home safe," Mr. Swallow said.

"What am I going to tell Momma?" Flo asked.

"Tell her I needed to play the piano," Daddy replied. "She'll understand."

As they headed for the door, Flo thought of something else. "Daddy," she said, "don't play cards."

He gave her a puzzled look. "I'm going to play the piano, Flo."

Mr. Swallow knew what she meant, though. He winked at Flo and said, "Just the piano."

Chapter 13
Playing for An Angel

Momma was furious when Flo told her what had happened. "The doctor said that man has got to keep off his foot," she said. "If he doesn't, it might not heal right."

"When he's playing the piano, though, he'll be sitting down," Flo said.

"In a jazz club, of all places," Momma went on. "Did they tell you what club?"

"No, only that it was just a couple of blocks away."

"I wish I knew where he was," Momma said. "I'd go right down there and drag him out. That's what I get for letting a jazz musician board here."

After the children went to bed, Flo could hear Momma walking back and forth in the living room. Finally Flo got up. Momma was looking out the window at the street.

"Momma, you need your sleep too," Flo said. "They probably won't be home till late."

"How can I sleep?" Momma said. "Your daddy is out somewhere I don't even know about. Can hardly walk. How could he do such a fool thing?"

"Momma," Flo said, "you know how much Daddy loves to play the piano."

Momma looked out the window again. "Yes, I know, Flo. It's in his heart to do it. But if we'd only stayed in Mississippi, he could play the piano every Sunday."

"Momma, we're all so much better off here in Chicago."

"I guess so. You and Toby are, and Bubber too. It's a chance for you to get somewhere."

"Won't you go to bed, Momma?"

"I'll just wait up for a little while longer," she said. "You get your rest."

Flo finally fell asleep. In the morning, she could smell breakfast cooking. She got up to find Momma in the kitchen. The two other bedroom doors were shut.

"Don't make any noise," Momma told her. "Your daddy is sleeping."

"Were you awake when they came in?" Flo asked.

"I was asleep on the couch, but he woke me."

"Did they give him the job?" Flo asked.

"Playing in the band? Of course they did. Who wouldn't want your daddy? He's just about the best piano player anybody ever heard."

"Well, Momma, then maybe that's the job Daddy should have."

"That's what he told me. And you know what? He wanted me to quit my job."

"You could, if Daddy's making money."

"Dear Flo, you know how long a musician's job lasts?" Momma snapped her fingers. "Long as that. You ever notice they have a new band playing every week in that Onion Club?"

"I guess so." Flo was surprised Momma paid attention to who was playing at the Onion Club.

"Besides," said Momma, "I like my job, to tell the truth. Look at what I brought home yesterday." She put a plate of sweet rolls with icing in front of Flo.

Flo checked the mailbox when she got home that afternoon. There was a letter in it! But when she took it out, she saw it was for Daddy. The return address in the corner of the envelope showed that it was from Reverend James.

She took it upstairs, but forgot about it when she saw Daddy. He was wearing a new suit–dark blue with a light blue stripe, and a tie and shirt to match.

"What do you think?" Daddy asked, standing up.

"Keen!" Toby said. That was a new word that had been going around school.

"It's beautiful, Daddy," Flo said. "You look so different."

"Had a little trouble getting the pants over my foot," he said. "But I wiggled through. As soon as that foot's better, I'll buy some new shoes too."

"Where did you get the money?" Flo asked. She knew that was what Momma's first question would be.

"The band leader gave me an advance on my first week's salary. He said I had to look right for the club."

"What club is it?"

"The DeLuxe."

"And what's the name of your band?"

"Major Parker's Sweet New Orleans Seven."

Flo laughed. "Daddy, you've never been to New Orleans."

"We'll teach him to play New Orleans style," said Mr. Swallow. "Your daddy does have the gift."

"Oh, that reminds me," Flo said. "A letter came for you."

Daddy opened it and began to read. All the happiness went out of his face. "What's the matter, Daddy?" Flo asked.

He just handed her the letter. The words jumped out at her. Aunt Lil had died.

"Oh, Daddy," Flo said. "I'm so sorry."

He shook his head. "Just when things go up a little, something else brings you down. I was sort of hoping that someday I could save the money to bring her up to Chicago too."

Flo didn't say it, but she thought Aunt Lil would never have wanted to leave Mississippi.

"I think I'll just go in the bedroom and lie down for a little while," Daddy said.

While Flo made breakfast for Mr. Swallow, she told him how much Aunt Lil meant to Daddy. "She taught him to play the piano," Flo said.

"Did a good job of it," he replied.

"When you said he had the gift, I thought of her. That's what she always says–said."

After he ate, Mr. Swallow began to get ready to leave for the club. He knocked on the bedroom door and said, "We got to go, Bill."

Daddy came out. His eyes were red. "I don't think I'm up to playing tonight."

Mr. Swallow hesitated. "Well, I understand your grief, Bill, but the Major isn't going to appreciate that. And you already bought that suit with his money."

Daddy looked down as if he'd forgotten he was wearing the new suit. "Maybe I could take it back," he said.

"Daddy," Flo said, "Aunt Lil would want you to play the piano tonight."

"You think so?"

"She always loved to hear you play. You know that. She's in heaven now, and she'll hear you."

Daddy kind of smiled a little. "Maybe that's right." He looked at Mr. Swallow. "I'm going to play kind of loud tonight."

"Make the angels sit up and listen," said Mr. Swallow.

After they'd gone, Toby said, "Why don't we go down to the DeLuxe Club and try to get in? I know where it is."

"Toby, Momma would have a fit. And what about Bubber?"

"Well, let's take him and just go look at the outside anyway," Toby said. "That can't hurt, and we'll be back before Momma even gets home."

It was just beginning to get dark out. No one was

going inside the DeLuxe Club yet. People didn't start coming to clubs till late at night. But the electric sign outside was on—so bright they could see it from a block away.

On the front of the club was a big poster: "Now Playing! Major Parker's Sweet New Orleans Seven!" It showed Major Parker holding a baton. He was a big heavy man with gold rings on both hands.

"Someday we'll see a poster with Daddy on it," Toby said.

Flo smiled and said, "I hope so." She wanted to stay till the band started to play, but the doorman came out and shooed them away.

Two weeks after Daddy started to play with the band, Flo came home to find Mr. Swallow packing his suitcase. "Are you leaving?" she said.

"The job here is over," he said. "Major has booked us into a club in New York. Second-best city in the world."

Flo remembered when he had said that about Chicago. Suddenly, she realized what that meant. "Is Daddy going with you?"

His voice came from behind her. "No, Flo, don't worry. I'm staying in Chicago."

Mr. Swallow shook his head. "You're making a mistake, Bill. It's a chance for the big time."

"That kind of life isn't for me," Daddy said. Flo could tell from his voice, though, that he wished he were going.

As Mr. Swallow got set to leave, Daddy said, "I'll wrap up your records for you."

"Naw, keep 'em," Mr. Swallow said. "They're just extra baggage. Maybe I'll send you another when the band makes one. There's big money in records. That's the wave of the future."

He gave Flo a salute when he went out the door. "You're a great cook, Flo. Open a restaurant and I'll come back."

Chapter 14
The Prize

Daddy's spirits fell after Mr. Swallow left. He stayed in the apartment most of the time, listening to jazz records. But even the music didn't cheer him up. He just sat on the couch, moving his hands as if he were playing the piano.

Momma started to worry. One night she told him, "Bill, if you feel so bad, why don't you find another piano job?"

Flo jumped up and hugged her. "Well," Momma said, "just till his foot's better and he can go back to his real job."

"It's not so easy," Daddy said. "All the bands have piano players better than me."

"Stop that talk," Momma said. "Nobody is better than you."

"Daddy," said Flo. "Remember what Mr. Swallow said about records? Why don't you make a record?"

He smiled sadly. "You got to be famous for that. Or pay for it yourself, and hope that enough people buy the record."

"How much does it cost?" Flo asked.

"Too much," he said. "There's a place called Black Swan Records on Thirty-fifth Street. Claude Swallow told me you could make a record there for twenty-five dollars."

"Don't even think about that," said Momma.

But Flo was thinking about it. Twenty-five dollars was the first prize in the *Defender's* story contest. It had been so long now that she had almost given up hope.

That night, though, she prayed to Aunt Lil. "This is Daddy's chance, Aunt Lil. Help me win the contest, please."

The next day, Flo screamed when she opened the mailbox and found a letter. The envelope had *Chicago Defender* printed on it.

"What happened?" Toby asked as Flo tore it open. "Did somebody else die?"

"No!" she told him. "Aunt Lil answered my prayer."

But the letter didn't say Flo had won first prize. It said she had won a prize in the story contest. A prize. Not the prize. Flo knew there was a difference.

Still, it was exciting to win something. The letter

told her to come to the *Defender's* office on Saturday for her prize.

Flo asked Momma and Daddy to go with her. They could hardly believe it, because Flo had never told them she entered the contest. When they read the letter, Momma said, "I'll treasure this till I die."

"What's the prize going to be?" asked Toby.

"I don't know," Flo said. "I hoped—" but she didn't finish, because she didn't want to disappoint them.

"The letter says your story will be printed in the *Defender*," Daddy said. "That's prize enough for me. I'll send a copy of it to everybody in Parkersville."

On Saturday, the whole family went along to see Flo collect her prize. Daddy wore his new suit, and Momma slipped her arm through his as they walked along the street. She really was proud of him, Flo thought.

Upstairs, a secretary showed them into a big room where people were sitting on folding chairs. Flo looked around and counted nine other boys and girls with their families.

A well-dressed man with a mustache stood up and began to speak. "I am Robert Abbott, the editor of the *Defender*," he said. "Our newspaper is proud today to recognize so many talented young people of our race. The words you have written, published in the *Defender,* will give hope to others still in the South. Through you, they will know that a better life awaits them if they find the courage to try."

Flo squeezed Momma's hand. Momma nodded. She got the message.

"And now," Mr. Abbott said, "To present the awards, let me introduce Ida Wells, a woman who has long led the fight for equality and justice."

Flo had read about Ida Wells. The *Defender* had printed many articles about her. She had edited her own newspaper in Tennessee, but white people closed it down. After that happened, she moved to Chicago, where she started an organization to help Negroes in the South.

"I was one of the judges for this contest," Mrs. Wells said. "It was a difficult job, because there were so many entries that deserved a prize. I am truly impressed. These stories show that our new generation is a bright hope for the future." She looked around. "Your families, I know, share that hope. Remember always that their struggle, their efforts, have helped to pave the way for your success."

Flo's heart was bursting as Mrs. Wells read off the name of the first-prize winner. It wasn't hers. It was a boy who looked a lot older than she was. Flo forced herself to applaud as he went forward to receive a white envelope from Mrs. Wells. Flo stared at the envelope, knowing that there was twenty-five dollars inside.

"And now, the runners-up," said Mrs. Wells. "Mr. Abbott has generously agreed to give each of you a prize too."

She started to read the names. Flo's was fourth, and as she walked forward, her family clapped and cheered. Mrs. Wells shook her hand and gave her an envelope.

When Flo returned to her seat, Toby leaned across Momma. "What is it?" he asked. "Open it!"

Flo lifted the flap of the envelope. Inside was a five-dollar bill. As she handed it to Toby, tears began to flow from her eyes.

"Wow!" Toby said. "We can buy some more records now."

Momma could tell something was wrong, though. "Flo!" she whispered. "You ought to be happy. Didn't you hear what these people said about you?"

Flo nodded and tried to smile. Daddy patted her on the back. "You're a winner, girl," he said.

After the awards were presented, Mr. Abbott and Mrs. Wells stayed to chat with each of the winners' families. Momma beamed as Mrs. Wells shook her hand.

Flo took a deep breath. "Mrs. Wells, I want to ask

you something," she said.

"Why, of course, Flo," replied Mrs. Wells.

"What do you think about jazz?"

Mrs. Wells looked surprised.

"Because," Flo explained, "my daddy is a jazz musician."

Daddy laughed and said, "Just a very part-time one."

"You didn't mention that in your story, Flo," said Mrs. Wells.

"He hadn't started to play for a band then," Flo explained. "But I want to know what you think of jazz."

"Why, I enjoy jazz," Mrs. Wells said. "It's our music. Music that comes from the soul of our race. It's one of our greatest creations."

Flo smiled. "Thank you, Mrs. Wells. That's better than any prize you could have given me."

On the way home, Momma took Flo aside and asked, "What were you crying about when you got that prize?"

"Momma, I don't want to tell you," Flo said.

"You shouldn't worry about not winning the first prize. What you won was almost as good."

"No, it wasn't," Flo said. "I wanted to win twenty-five dollars so I could pay for Daddy to make a record."

"I see," said Momma. "And what you asked Mrs. Wells—that was to help me understand. Is that it?"

Flo smiled. "I guess so."

"As if I didn't know," Momma said.

When they got home, Flo gave her prize money to Daddy. "Buy some more records with it," she said. "We'll all enjoy them."

Momma had gone into the bedroom to take off her hat. When she came out, she had something in her hand. It was money—one-dollar and five-dollar bills rolled up and tied with a string. She held it out to Daddy.

"This is twenty dollars," she said. "I'm putting it with Flo's prize so you can go down and make your record."

Nobody spoke for a moment. "Amelia," Daddy said finally, "where'd you get this money? Not from that job of yours?"

"No, you know all that's gone for rent and food. This is what's left from your army pay. I been saving it."

"What for? You want a new dress? You should have it."

"No," Momma said, shaking her head. "I saved this for train tickets back to Mississippi." She looked at Flo. "I guess we're not ever going back there now."

Flo put her arms around Momma. "You won't be sorry," Flo said.

"Hurry up and take this down to that Black Swan Records place," Momma told Daddy. "Or I'll change my mind."

Chapter 15
Lillian's Dream

The day after Flo's story appeared in the *Defender,* she showed it to Mrs. Kaufman. "Your parents must be proud," she told Flo. "And I have a surprise for you too. I want you to take the article down to Miss Underwood's office."

"Oh, I don't want to," Flo said.

"She's expecting you," Mrs. Kaufman said. "I showed her the copy you made for me."

Flo was scared as she walked down the hall. Ever since the first day, she had tried to keep as far away from Miss Underwood as possible. But as soon as she went in the door, Miss Underwood told her to sit down.

"I have read the story you wrote," she told Flo.

Flo nodded.

"Mrs. Kaufman told me you wrote it in her class without any help. Is that true?"

"Yes, ma'am. I wrote some at home too."

Miss Underwood folded her hands. "I believe I made a mistake at the beginning of the school year in sending you to second grade."

Flo's hair stood up on the back of her neck. She tried to sit very still.

"If you had attended school in Chicago, I would have placed you in sixth grade," said Miss Underwood. "Do you think you can do the work there?"

"I'll try my best, Miss Underwood."

"A good answer," said Miss Underwood. "You will start tomorrow."

Flo couldn't wait till Momma got home from her job to tell her. Daddy wasn't there in the afternoons anymore. He was practicing on a piano at the record company. He said he was writing a new song for his record.

Flo and Toby asked if they could go along to hear his recording session. "We never have heard you play jazz," Flo said. "And it's not a club, so Momma won't mind."

In fact, Momma surprised them all. She took the day off from work so she could listen too.

There couldn't be any noise in the recording room, so they all watched from behind a glass window. The man who operated the record machine was back there.

Daddy looked up at them from the piano. He pressed his fingers back, first one hand and then the other. Flo could see he was nervous. When the machine started, he had only one chance to make the record right.

They could hear his voice through a loudspeaker. "I wrote this song for Aunt Lil," he said. "I call it 'Lillian's Dream.' "

Daddy nodded to the operator, who flipped a switch and pointed to him.

Daddy's hands came down on the keyboard, playing a melody they all knew: "Roll, Jordan, Roll." For a second, Flo was disappointed, because Daddy said this was a new song.

But he knew what he was doing. He started to change the melody around. Daddy used the high treble notes to make a sound like train wheels turning. He switched keys and started to play faster. Another melody broke into the first–making a sound that reminded Flo of Chicago.

Flo glanced over at Momma. She had her eyes closed and was swaying back and forth, the way she did when Daddy played in church. Toby started to clap his hands to the rhythm of the music.

Near the end of the song, Daddy brought in the melody of "Roll, Jordan, Roll" again. But he played it like nobody ever had before.

Flo watched his hands fly across the keyboard, and now she understood the secret of jazz at last. It was about freedom. Daddy's music was telling Aunt Lil, and everybody else, what it meant to be free.

Timeline

This timeline shows the major events of the African American migration to Chicago, and the beginning of the Jazz Age of the 1920s.

1908
Ferdinand "Jelly Roll" Morton and Tony Jackson, two African American musicians from New Orleans, begin to play jazz music in Chicago clubs.

1905
Robert S. Abbott starts the *Chicago Defender*.

1910–1920
African American population of Chicago increases from about 44,000 to about 109,000.

1905

1908

1909

1910

1911

1909
Ida B. Wells helps to found the National Association for the Advancement of Colored People (NAACP). The NAACP would lead the fight for racial justice for the next 50 years.

Ida B. Wells

1911
National Urban League founded. Its members in Northern cities helped newly arrived African Americans from the South.

Oscar de Priest

Race riot in Chicago
causes the deaths of
48 people. Afterward,
Robert Abbott becomes
part of a committee
dedicated to improving
race relations in
Chicago.

1919

1915

Oscar de Priest
becomes first African
American elected to
Chicago City Council.

1917

1915

1922

1917–1918

United States takes
part in World War I.
African American
soldiers fought in
some of the major
battles in France.

1922

Louis Armstrong
leaves New Orleans
for Chicago, where
he joins Joseph "King"
Oliver's jazz band.
Armstrong would
become the most
popular jazz musician
of his time.

1917

First recording of jazz
music made by the
Original Dixieland
Jazz Band.

Louis Armstrong

121

The True Story

The Great Migration of African Americans began around 1900. Bigotry and "Jim Crow" laws—which forced African Americans into second-class status—caused them to seek a better life in Northern states. They still faced prejudice in the North, but they could obtain better jobs and housing, and send their children to schools far better than the ones in the South. Both Ida B. Wells and Robert S. Abbott encouraged the migration of African Americans to the North.

Ida B. Wells was born on a Mississippi slave plantation in 1862. When she was 22, she became part-owner of a newspaper in Memphis, Tennessee. After she printed the names of a group of whites who had lynched three African Americans, a mob wrecked her newspaper office and its printing press.

Wells fled to New York and began a lifelong crusade against lynching. In 1894 she went to Chicago and a year later married Ferdinand L. Barnett, a lawyer. She helped found the National Association for the Advancement of Colored People in 1909. She also fought to win for women the right to vote. She became well-known as a lecturer in the United States and Europe, continuing to speak out for social justice until her death in 1931.

Robert S. Abbott

Robert S. Abbott was born in Georgia in 1870. After attending college, he moved to Chicago, where he founded the *Chicago Defender* in 1905. He exposed discrimination and lynchings, printing letters from readers with first-hand news. He continually advised his readers that African Americans could improve their condition by moving North. Many wrote to him asking for advice and help in making the move.

Abbott's newspaper was often passed from hand to hand throughout the South. By 1929, the circulation of the *Defender* was over 200,000. After Abbott's death in 1940, the *Defender* continued to be one of the most important and widely read black-owned newspapers.